Can YOU spot the spotted
frog hidden in the story?

For my Mother

Marie Burlington grew up near the sea at Sandymount, Dublin. After studying art in NCAD for a while, she worked in various jobs, including work as a draftswoman and freelance artist.

As her two children grew up, she started writing and illustrating children's books.

She illustrated *Trouble for Tuffy* in the Flyer series, then wrote and illustrated *Helpful Hannah* and *Lighthouse Joey* in the Panda series. Her last book *Dear Me*, is a diary for slightly older readers. She lives with her husband and family in Wicklow.

The Little Witch who can't spell

Marie Burlington

THE O'BRIEN PRESS
DUBLIN

First published 2008 by The O'Brien Press Ltd,
12 Terenure Road East, Rathgar, Dublin 6, Ireland.
Tel: +353 1 4923333; Fax: +353 1 4922777
E-mail: books@obrien.ie
Website: www.obrien.ie

ISBN: 978-0-86278-982-4

British Library Cataloguing-in-Publication Data
A catalogue record for this title is available from
the British Library.

1 2 3 4 5 6 7 8 9 10
08 09 10 11 12

The O'Brien Press
receives assistance from

Layout and design: The O'Brien Press Ltd
Illustrations: Marie Burlington
Printed in the UK by CPI Bookmarque, Croydon, CR0 4TD

CHAPTER 1

Willow Witch

Willow Witch lives in a **haunted** house on top of Witchy Mountain.

She has a pet cat called **Spooky**,
who is her best friend in the whole,
wide world.

She goes to Cobwebs Junior School
where she has a **spell** book instead of
a spelling book.

There are lots of different types of spells.

There are:

smelly spells,

chilly spells,

fizzy spells

and

dizzy spells.

9

And many more.

Willow Witch sometimes **forgets** her spells.

Her backward ones go forward ...

and her forward ones go backward.

One day Willow was having trouble at school.

'No, no, no, Willow!' cackled Miss Wart, her teacher. 'That's **not** the way to spell.'

Willow was waving her wand all over the place and making a **magic mess**.

Miss Wart took her wand away.

'You'll get this back when you
learn to spell **properly**,' she cackled.

Spooky hid under the table. He was
afraid of Miss Wart.

'Miss Wart is a real **crosspatch**, Spooky,' said Willow later. 'Somehow I'll just have to prove I can do my spells.'

Spooky nodded sadly. He thought that might be a problem now that Willow had no wand.

CHAPTER 2

The Lost Wand

Later that day Chief Wizard (the most **important** wizard on Witchy Mountain) was out walking. He was making plans for the big Hallowe'en party. It was the most important event of the year for everyone on Witchy Mountain.

Chief Wizard was trying to think of recipes.

'Fiendish fries, monster muffins, scary sandwiches. Yum, yum,' he said to himself, drooling at the idea of the wonderful **goodies**.

The trouble was Chief Wizard couldn't cook at all and most of his goodies tasted more like baddies.

He sat down under a tree. It had just finished raining and the grass was still damp. Slowly his robes got wetter and wetter.

'Rusting **raindrops**,' he yelled as he jumped up. 'I should have worn my winter woolies.'

He got such a fright, he forgot to
pick up his wand.

'Brrr ...' he mumbled to himself,
feeling a bit **soggy**. 'I'd better get
home and warm myself by the fire.

CHAPTER 3

Magic Muddles

'It might be an idea to get some new **ingredients** for our spells,' said Willow to Spooky, who was snoozing happily in his basket.

'We're just going out, Mum,'
Willow shouted to her mum who was
busy setting **ghost-traps**. Now that it
was getting cold, there were more
ghosts than ever around the house.
(Ghosts like to spend the winter in
cosy walls or attics.)

Like the ghosts, Spooky didn't feel like going out in the cold.

'P-L-E-A-S-E,' begged Willow.

'Oh all right,' meowed Spooky **grumpily** and the two set out to see what they could find.

They found berries and bottles and bee-stings and buttons.

They found bat's whiskers, fishtails and tickles and toenails.

'Who knows when these might come in handy,' said Willow as she popped them into her basket.

Spooky wasn't so sure. Willow had lots of jars that went **POP** and **SPLAT** in her bedroom. What might happen if she added these ingredients?

'I think we have enough for now,' sighed Willow happily and they set off home.

As they were passing a tree, Spooky noticed something **sparkling** in the grass. He ran over.

'What is it, Spooky?' asked Willow.

'WOW,' she said when she saw it. 'A **beautiful** wand. I wonder who it belongs to. It looks like a real Wizard Wand. Perhaps we should see if it still works.'

24

This was a bad idea. A wizard's wand is full of **magic power**. And Willow's spells are *always* mixed up.

Mixed-up spells and magic power spell only one thing and that's **magic muddles**.

'Oh no!' thought Spooky. I sense
trouble.

They walked further along the road
until they met Gertrude Witch.

Willow hid the wand behind her
back.

'Hello, Willow,' said Gertrude. 'I'm
just on my way to the hairdresser.'

Gertrude had fallen off her broom one day and she'd got such a **fright** her hair's been standing on end ever since.

Hmmm ... I just might be able to help, thought Willow. She waved the wand ...

WHOOSH … went the wand as it twirled round and round. Stars **sparkled** at its tip.

'I wonder if I can think of a spell,' said Willow.

Eye of bat and flowery twig!
Make Gertrude's hair as nice as a wig.
Soft and pretty as can be.
Wild flowers on top for all to see.

Spooky **dived** for cover in the long grass.

'AAAAH!' screamed Gertrude as huge flowers grew out of her hair which looked like a strange wig.

'**Cool.**' Willow smiled to herself as Gertrude ran around the corner. 'No more bad hair days for Gertrude. I must see if I can do some more wonderful magic,' she said.

'Nooo,' meowed Spooky, but it was no good. He could feel one of his nine lives slipping away.

Further on down the road Willow saw Wally Warlock trying to learn his spelling. He had reached the letter D.

Now Wally was very good at **spells** but he didn't like spelling.

I'm sure I can help, thought Willow. She waved the wand.

'Oh no,' meowed Spooky, running for cover in the bushes.

WHOOSH ... went the wand as it twirled round and round. Stars **sparkled** at its tip.

Numbers, letters, alphabet soup.
Squiggles, scribbles, scrabble loop.
Make Wally's words all spell
together.
Written high in cloudy weather.

Wally's book flew out of his hands and up into the **sky**. The pages flew open in the wind.

Letters fell out. They spelt out lots of silly words all beginning with the letter **D**.

Dillybird.
Drizzlemoon.
Dragon burp
Dribbledrop

Amazing, thought Willow. I've invented a whole new **language**.

'Aaaah!' wailed Wally. 'Those aren't real words,' he cried as he ran off. 'I'm telling Miss Wart!'

'Oh no,' said Willow to Spooky

'I'll really be in **trouble** then.
I think I'd better get this wand to
Chief Wizard. He'll know what to do
with it.'

Thank goodness, thought Spooky,
crawling out from under the hedge.

CHAPTER 4

More Magic Muddles

Chief Wizard was warming his bones by the fire. He was just feeling a bit better when he heard a knock on the door.

RAT A TAT, TAT!

'Who could that be?' he wondered.
'A wizard can't get a minute's **peace**
around here.'

He opened the door and looked
down.

There, looking a bit guilty, was a
small witch holding a **BIG** wand.

'Well, well, well,' he boomed.
'What have we here?'

Willow tried to explain. Spooky hid
behind her.

Down the road Chief Wizard could see an angry Miss Wart with Gertrude and Wally making their way to his house.

'You'd better wait in the kitchen,' he said. 'I think I see **trouble** coming up the road.'

Willow and Spooky ran into the kitchen.

Spooky jumped into an open **cupboard**. Willow closed the door behind him.

There was a **BIG cauldron** underneath the cupboard. Willow climbed in and tried to hide. She still had the wand in her hand.

Inside the cauldron was a long list of Chief Wizard's **recipes** for Hallowe'en.

'Maybe I can help,' she whispered loudly to Spooky as he put his paws over his ears.

'Not again!' he meowed.

Willow climbed out of the cauldron and put in the ingredients from her basket.

She **stirred** and **stirred**.

She **whisked** and **whirred**.

She could hear Miss Wart at the door, cackling at the top of her voice.

She waved the wand ...

WHOOSH ... went the wand as it twirled round and round.

Stars **sparkled** at its tip.

Spooky tried to hide behind some bags of flour in the cupboard.

Make dazzling dishes and dainty delights!

Toasty and crispy with treats that taste right.

So yummy and scrummy you'll lick the plate clean.

With a pumpkin the like that's never been seen.

Something started to **sizzle**.

Something started to **stink**.

Something started to **stir**.

Spooky tried to run for it.

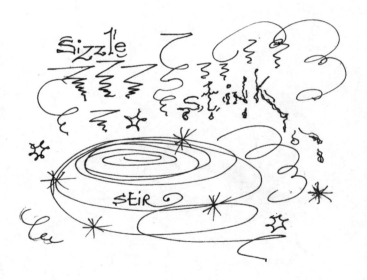

The cupboard door flew open.

The bags of flour fell into the
sizzling mix.

Then **Spooky** fell in too.

'HELP!' he meowed, but it was too
late.

CHAPTER 5

The Best Hallowe'en Ever

Chief Wizard was doing his best to calm everyone down. He took out his spare wand and fixed Gertrude's hair. It looked better than ever.

Gertrude looked in the mirror and was **delighted**.

He gave Wally Warlock a new
spelling book, which was **magic**. The
book could speak to Wally, to help
him learn his spellings.

The only one Chief Wizard couldn't help was Miss Wart, who was **cackling** away and getting more and more angry.

Then they heard the **noise** in the kitchen.

They heard **whizbangs** and **wallops**.

They heard **smashing** and **sizzling**.

They heard **whirling** and **twirling**.

They all started to get a bit worried.

They tried the door handle, but it wouldn't open.

So they all tried it together.

Just then everything stopped.

It suddenly went very quiet.

They gave the door one last **BIG** push.

It flew open.

They fell into the room.

As they watched, cakes and goodies of every kind landed on the table.

There were all the **wonderful** things that Chief Wizard had wanted and a few more besides.

They were:

mummified marshmallows,

ghoulish grapes,

petrified pancakes

and ...

rotting rasberry milkshakes

and lots more ...

Right in the middle was a beautiful

BIG pumpkin.

On top sat **Spooky,** looking very
pleased with himself.

'Well, well, well,' said Chief Wizard. 'What wonderful goodies. It seems Willow Witch can get something **right** after all. What do you think, Miss Wart?'

For the first time in her life Miss Wart just couldn't think of **anything** to say at all.

Chief Wizard wrote down all the
ingredients.

Willow Witch wrote down the
spell and for the first Hallowe'en ever
all the goodies tasted very good
indeed.

In fact, everything worked out so well that Miss Wart gave Willow her **wand** back.

Even Spooky enjoyed himself as everyone thought he looked **wonderful** sitting on top of the biggest pumpkin they had ever seen.

The whole of Witchy Mountain agreed it was the **best** Hallowe'en anyone could remember, ever.

Especially Willow!